A Practical Guide to
Vampires

Compiled by

Treval Vorgard

Vampire Enthusiast and Occasional Hunter

MIRRORSTONE

VAMPIRE BASICS

They haunt the streets at midnight and roam abandoned homes. They charm even those most skeptical of magic, and they inspire fear, while at the same time inspiring curiosity. I'm talking, of course, about vampires.

Vampires are formed by the bite of another vampire. Most victims are unwilling. But I have heard stories of foolish mortals who seek out vampires in order to become one themselves. In my years of research, one fact has become certain: vampires are a most elusive race of monsters, and no one has any clear idea just how many hide among us.

As much as I find vampires fascinating, I would highly discourage such reckless behavior! The consequences are far too great.

After meeting my first vampire, and every vampire thereafter, I put together a list of vampire characteristics to help me recognize a vampire in the future.

HOW TO RECOGNIZE A VAMPIRE

If you're unsure if you have met a vampire, look for the following characteristics:

1. Pale skin. You can almost see the veins through the skin!

2. No shadow and no reflection.

3. Mostly active at night.

4. Eyes with a reddish cast. Green or blue irises.

5. Thick, healthy hair.

6. A person who suddenly appears and/or suddenly vanishes, without warning or prelude.

You will also NOT see any blemishes or wrinkles.

Vampires don't cast shadows, and they avoid mirrors.

Some vampires have been known to grow hair on their palms!

Vampire Anatomy

Vampires belong to the class of monsters known as the undead. They are not technically alive, but they do resemble living beings. When we take a close look at vampire anatomy, we can see these monsters share many characteristics of the human body, but there are some telling differences.

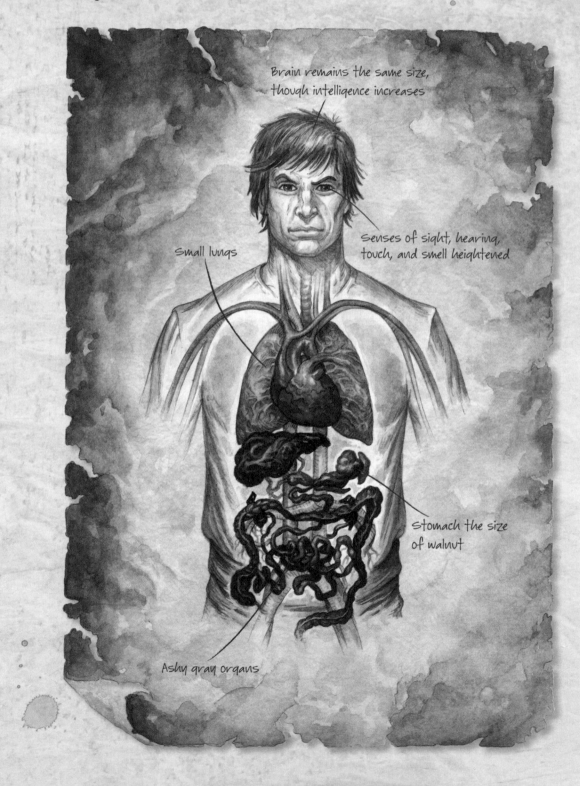

Brain remains the same size, though intelligence increases

Senses of sight, hearing, touch, and smell heightened

Small lungs

Stomach the size of walnut

Ashy gray organs

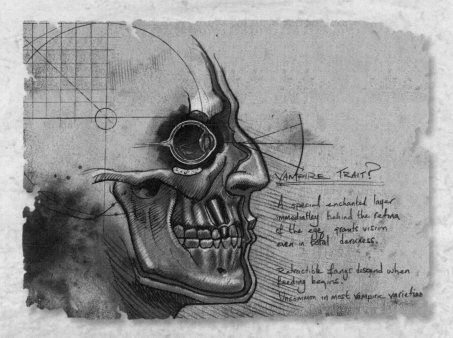

VAMPIRE TRAIT?

A special enchanted layer immediatley behind the retina of the eye grants vision even in total darkness.

Retractible fangs descend when feeding begins. Uncommon in most vampiric varieties

This transformation is known as "being turned" and the date on which it occurs serves as a vampire's "birthday."

A vampire has lungs, but it does not use them for breathing oxygen. A vampire can live for days in a closed crypt, and it can sometimes even survive under the sea. A vampire has lungs only to provide air for its speech. Therefore, its lungs are somewhat smaller than an average human's lungs.

A vampire's heart still pumps blood, and the fluid travels through a vampire's veins in much the same way as a human's. But the vampire's blood does not absorb anything as it passes through the lungs. This means that a vampire remains immune to any toxic chemicals or poisons in the air. Vampire's blood also has one characteristic quality: when viewed through a light source, it's not red, but a shimmery shade of gold.

Caution: Use care when handling vampire blood. It can burn like acid or explode in certain circumstances.

Most vampires do not partake in solid food, so their digestive system serves little purpose. When a mortal becomes a vampire, the stomach shrivels to the size of a walnut, and the other digestive organs wither to a distinct ashy gray color.

A vampire's nervous system remains largely unaltered from that of its mortal state. However, its hearing, touch, and sense of smell gain heightened sensitivity. A vampire also develops the power to see in absolute darkness.

A vampire's teeth are undoubtedly its most distinct feature. When a vampire is turned, its canine teeth sharpen and lengthen. These teeth have evolved to be retractable, allowing vampires to move more freely among human society.

The length and sharpness varies from vampire to vampire.

A recently fed vampire

It goes without saying that these vampires are the most dangerous of all!

A vampire may also drink animal blood if no other option is available.

Vampires and Food

Vampires gain nutrients by consuming blood. Conventional wisdom will have you believe that vampires feast only on human blood, and it is true that this food source is the most nutritious for the undead body. But my years of research and exploration have revealed numerous vampires who avoid human blood for moral and ethical reasons. Ironically known among themselves as "vegetarian" vampires, these creatures prefer animal blood to satisfy their nutritional needs.

A vampire prefers to feed at least once a day. One can easily identify a recently fed vampire by its pinkish skin and energetic demeanor. In contrast, a starving vampire will take on a very pale cast and behave quite sluggishly.

While they cannot gain any nutrients from solid food, some vampires do choose to continue a normal human diet, partaking in all the same tasty delights that they enjoyed before they were turned. Their bodies are unable to extract any nutrition from the food they eat, but they keep up the practice because they continue to enjoy the taste of their favorite dishes and the custom of eating three meals a day. If solid food is not regularly introduced into the vampire's body, over time, its system will reject the food involuntarily. In this case, if a vampire attempts even a mere bite of bread, it will vomit.

Many vampires who eat solid foods also do so to maintain the illusion of being human, as they wish to keep their vampiric identity a secret.

Unfortunately, I have been a witness to such an event. It was quite disgusting!

Known Vampire Allergens

Vampires cannot properly digest solid foods, and for that reason poisons and magic elixirs cannot affect them. However if any of the following do happen to pass a vampire's lips, the vampire may weaken and fall ill, similar to an allergic reaction in a human. If you attempt to use any of these items in combat with a vampire, use extreme caution. The effects (if any) remain specific to individual vampires and are highly unpredictable.

Holly	Rice
Yew leaves	Silver
Rose petals	Mistletoe
Salt	Lilies

These items may also cause allergic reaction upon contact with a vampire's skin.

A starving vampire

Vampire Powers

At the moment a vampire is turned, its body instantly alters, and it develops a number of astonishing powers. To mortals, these powers seem caused by spellcraft, but in fact they are simply part of a vampire's natural state.

Vampires live for hundreds, if not thousands of years. And each year, a vampire's powers grow stronger. A newly turned vampire has less than half the strength of an older, patriarch vampire. No scholar has yet determined the reason for this. The most plausible theory is that a vampire's powers are so enormous, it takes years to learn how to master them. Only with time is a vampire able to develop the necessary willpower and focus to take full advantage of its supernatural skills.

This theory, of course, is one I developed myself!

Never forget: a vampire's powers (and its weaknesses) vary widely depending on the individual. Many a vampire hunter has fallen after having made false assumptions about a vampire enemy. Study any vampire you wish to confront very carefully before making any move.

Strength

Even from a very young age, vampires are notoriously strong. They can lift much heavier items than a mortal can, which is one reason why vampires are such deadly foes. Once vampires have a grip on their prey, it will be nearly impossible for the victims to break free. In addition, vampires can lift and toss victims through the air.

A fledgling vampire runs as fast as a fit human, while a patriarch vampire can run as quickly as a racehorse.

A vampire's talent for climbing is sometimes called spider climb.

Speed and Movement

Vampires are also very fast. By the time you realize that you are in the presence of a vampire, it is probably too late to run. A vampire can definitely outrace a mere mortal. In fact, the vampire might move so fast and so suddenly, it appears as though the vampire has disappeared.

Vampires are also very adept at climbing and swinging and leaping. They can flip in the air and scale the sides of cliffs or buildings with ease. The older the vampire, the more nimble it becomes.

Intelligence

Vampires are known as one of the most intelligent classes of monsters, capable of extreme cunning in achieving their goals. Upon being turned, a vampire will experience a sensation not unlike a severe headache, as its brain capacity instantly expands. After a few hours, the pain subsides; and from then on, the vampire's intelligence grows greater each night.

Although the brain does not appear to change in size.

Vampires often find that a clever plan, alongside their natural charm, is enough to achieve their aims, and they will always choose an intelligent scheme before resorting to brute force. Beware this most of all, when hunting or researching vampires. They are capable of setting ingenious traps and creating clever disguises. They can easily blend into human society where they instinctively identify personality weaknesses and turn humans against one another. They manipulate others to ensnare victims and carry out their evil plans.

Charm

Perhaps because of their supernatural intelligence, vampires have an indelible charm that factors into almost any scheme they engage in. A vampire lures its victim with the promise of a friendly supper or a fireside chat. Never, I repeat, never allow yourself to look directly into the eyes of a vampire. A vampire's hypnotic stare has the near-spell-like ability to leave you practically incapable of independent thought. Even a simple conversation with a vampire can pose a danger, for the monsters are so persuasive they can convince you to do anything.

Magic

A vampire's gaze and its charm are, indeed, very spell-like. Yet in actuality, the only vampires that are really able to conjure spells are vampires that had magical powers before they were turned. Their skills in casting spells traveled with them into the undead world, and very often, these powers became enhanced. If it is your desire to confront a vampire, be sure you know its mortal history before you do so!

Unless you wish to become a vampire yourself one day!

Shapeshifting

Vampires possess the power to change their form. They use this ability to protect themselves in combat, to travel long distances, or to take an enemy by surprise.

Mist Form

This moment of transformation is one of the few times such undead are extremely vulnerable to attack.

The most elusive form that a vampire can take on is that of a vapor. The process of transformation takes only a minute. Once in its mist form, a vampire is safe from any form of attack. In this form, a vampire can actually control the type of mist it takes on. It could become a thick, white cloud, or a nearly transparent vapor.

Animal Form

Vampires typically change into two types of creatures: bats or wolves. The choice depends both on the individual personality of the vampire and which form would best suit the situation it finds itself in. A vampire may choose to become a bat if it needs to fly out of reach of a vampire hunter or another vampire that might want to harm it. A wolf, on the other hand, is a much more accepted and deadly shape if the vampire is traversing through a forest. The wolf form also proves quite useful in combat.

HOW TO TELL?

How can we tell, then, if an animal is actually a vampire? Unfortunately, in most cases, you will not be able to identify the difference between a normal animal and a vampire in animal form. The traits of the animal itself and a vampire in animal form are nearly identical. Your only hope is to pay close attention to the animal's size. A vampire in bat or wolf form tends to be slightly larger than a normal animal of that species.

The Sun and Light

Most vampires will do everything in their power to avoid sunlight. Even cloudy days provide a hardship for vampires, for the strong sunbeams still find ways to the pale skin. That is why you rarely—if ever—see vampires walking about during the day.

If a vampire does, for some reason, need to be out during the daylight hours, it will take every precaution to avoid the sun, from wearing dark cloaks and hats, to restricting its movements to shaded alleys and underground passageways. The sun is not just an annoyance. It actually causes the vampire great pain. Unlike humans, a vampire does not merely get a sunburn. Instead, its pale, ivory skin will start to smoke, and depending on the sun's strength, the vampire's skin might even erupt into flames.

As vampires age, they become more able to tolerate sunlight for longer and longer periods of time, and the oldest vampires grow completely immune to its effects.

The sun, therefore, can be a good protection against vampires!

These terms are useful categories for vampire enthusiasts and hunters. Note that no vampire would ever use one of these terms directly in conversation with another vampire.

Vampire Ages

Age	Name
0–99 years	Fledgling
00–199 years	Mature
200–299 years	Old
300–399 years	Very Old
400–499 years	Ancient
500–999 years	Eminent
1000+ years	Patriarch

Vampires are known as patriarchs regardless of their gender. So a female vampire would still be known as a patriarch.

See Vampires in Combat for more information.

Immortality

Like all undead creatures, vampires are immortal. But while they will never grow old and die a natural death, their life-force can be destroyed by other, more specific means. A vampire maintains the appearance of the mortal age it was when it was turned, but this appearance has no bearing on the vampire's actual age. You may encounter a thousand-year-old vampire child, or a gray-haired fledgling vampire. As time goes on, a vampire does not experience any of the normal changes associated with aging: its skin will never wrinkle; its hair will not turn gray. As a vampire ages, however, its powers and cunning grow stronger. Therefore, before you attempt to combat or investigate any vampire, you would be well advised to first determine its age.

The Vampire Asleep

When the night draws to a close, vampires instinctively know they must find a safe place to rest.

Often the vampire prefers to sleep with a token from its mortal life. This token may be dirt taken from the vampire's original home, a piece of jewelry, or its own coffin. Many vampires believe that if they do not have this token when sleeping, they will be destroyed. However, there is no record of any such event every occurring. Some say it is merely a superstition.

If a vampire is awakened during daylight hours, it may suffer some dizziness and disorientation. It may be temporarily weakened. However, it does not take long for the vampire to recover its tremendous powers.

All vampire hunters must use caution when approaching the lair of a sleeping vampire. While this may seem like the safest time to attack a vampire, the risks are still extremely high. When sleeping, many vampires are still partially aware of their own surroundings and can sense danger approaching. Cunning as always, a vampire may even fake sleep to lure a vampire hunter to approach it, only to surprise the hunter with a vicious attack.

Although a coffin is a traditional resting place for a vampire, almost any comfortable, secure location will do.

Vampire Asleep	Vampire in Hibernation
Awakens each sunset or when disturbed	Cannot control when it wakes
Sleeps only in daylight hours	Sleeps for forty to hundreds of years
Can wake to fight a vampire hunter	Are in danger from vampire hunters
May fake sleep to surprise a hunter	Do not wake instantly
Typically sleeps in coffin	Sleeps surrounded by rock or earth

Typically a catacombs but some vampires excavate their own hibernation sites within graveyards or near their lairs.

Hibernation

If vampires are immortal, why is the world not overrun with patriarch vampires? The answer is somewhat surprising. Immortality can be a difficult burden for creatures as intelligent as vampires. With all the time in the world, a vampire can sometimes run out of things to do, and after many centuries, it simply grows bored.

So how do these creatures deal with their boredom? They go into a state of hibernation. Now, this hibernation is not a deep sleep, or even a half sleep. It is not for one night, or even for several nights. An older vampire who enters a state of hibernation may sleep for several decades, or even as much as an entire century! The vampire must adequately feed before it can hibernate, otherwise it might starve while it sleeps for so long. In addition, the older vampire must find a place that will not be disturbed for many years. A tomb or a cave or even a hollow beneath the body of a person already buried in a graveyard are all common hibernation locations.

Do not be fooled! A hibernating vampire may still be able to rouse itself if attacked by a vampire hunter.

VAMPIRE LIFE

Although they've long left the world of human ambition, vampires spend their nights engaged in fulfilling pursuits. When they are not charming their next victims or concocting a diabolical plan, they enjoy life as only vampires can, cataloguing their vast hoards of riches, collecting magic items, and becoming masters of whatever hobbies might suit their fancies.

Most of all, vampires enjoy caring for their opulent lairs. Vampires select homes that have a sense of death or destruction about them. The most traditional home for a vampire is, of course, a crumbling castle. Most castles are difficult to enter, often perched atop a rocky cliff or standing alone. Castles are imposing and do not welcome unexpected visitors. In such abodes, vampires remain safe. Vampires also seek abandoned manors as lairs, and enjoy living in any building or structure near a cemetery.

Hunting, though an important part of vampire life, cannot fill all the hours of the night. Vampires grow bored much more quickly than their human counterparts and need many activities to keep themselves amused.

HOW TO RECOGNIZE A VAMPIRE LAIR

1. A deserted, abandoned, or crumbling structure.

2. Bats or wolves seen in the vicinity.

3. Near a graveyard or other location of despair.

4. Occasional sightings of undead monsters nearby.

5. An unusual mist sometimes surrounds the area.

6. Entrance is secluded and dark.

7. A gargoyle guards the door.

8. Visitors enter but never leave the building.

The monster, not the statue

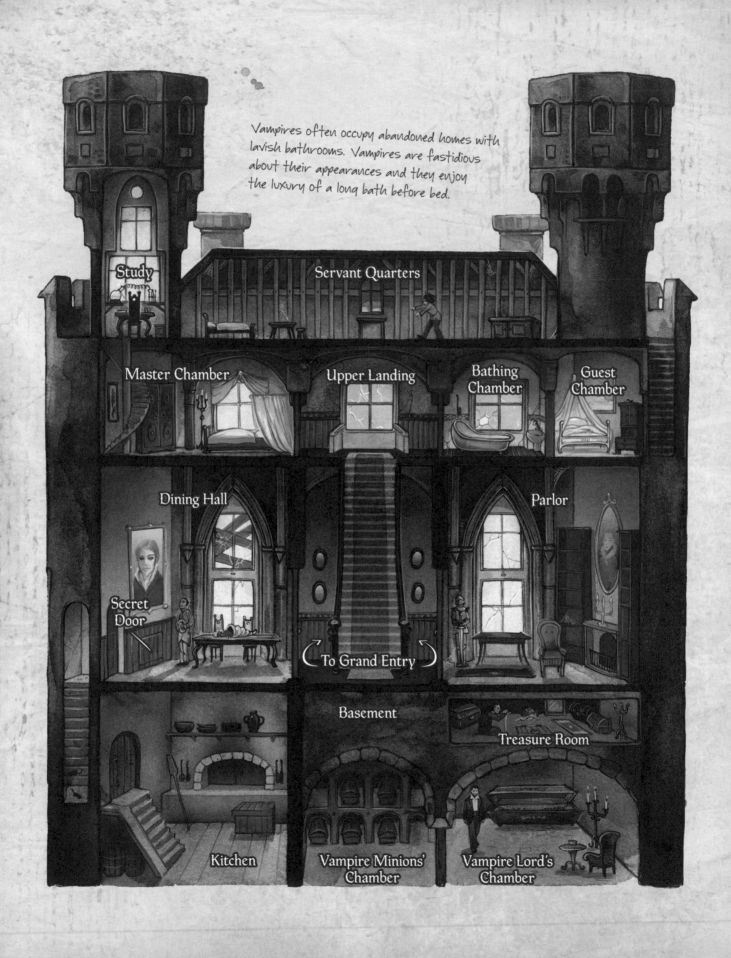

Vampires often occupy abandoned homes with lavish bathrooms. Vampires are fastidious about their appearances and they enjoy the luxury of a long bath before bed.

Study

Servant Quarters

Master Chamber

Upper Landing

Bathing Chamber

Guest Chamber

Dining Hall

Parlor

Secret Door

To Grand Entry

Basement

Treasure Room

Kitchen

Vampire Minions' Chamber

Vampire Lord's Chamber

Inside a Vampire's Lair

If you ever find yourself crossing the threshold of a vampire's lair, you'll notice several telling details that will confirm you have entered a vampire home. First and foremost, a vampire's lair is always filled with the best furnishings available. Vampires love antique furniture, expensive artwork, and lavish rugs and linens. Often vampires gather these items from their unfortunate victims, and they have been known to select targets just because their prey possess a coveted painting or chair.

A vampire's master chambers will look pristine, with no signs of anyone ever having stepped in the room. This is, of course, because the vampire never sleeps in this chamber. Instead, it rests in pure darkness in a room hidden somewhere in the home's basement or other underground storage areas. A vampire usually creates a room near its coffin to store its treasure, should any intruder try to rob its hoard while it sleeps. The kitchen is also rarely used. The stove is almost always covered in dust and cobwebs, for the vampire has no need to prepare food, unless it is entertaining guests.

All mirrors, of course—if they are in the vampire's home at all—will be covered with tapestries or turned to face the wall.

Excepting of course those vampires who have chosen to maintain their ability to eat human food. Those vampires often have a full kitchen staffed by zombies.

Gargoyle [monstrous humanoid]. A gargoyle looks like a statue perched above the threshold of a vampire's, wizard's, or other magic-user's dwelling. Originally, these beasts were simply decorative elements serving to funnel rain away from ancient buildings, but a resourceful sorcerer created a spell that brought them to life, and now they serve as guards all around the world. The gargoyle often serves as a guard to a vampire's lair and swoops down to defend its master's entrance from any unwanted guests.

Sometimes members of a vampire family group will adorn themselves with a matching piece of jewelry. The piece may come in many forms—button, medallion, belt buckle—and the symbol identifies allegiance to a particular vampire lord.

Vampire Society

In general, vampires are solitary creatures, much too selfish and territorial to ever consider sharing their lives with another of their kind. Although vampires enjoy seeking out mortals and engaging them in charming conversation, when meeting with another vampire, they cannot hide their jealous disdain and often refuse to speak at all.

You won't be surprised to learn, then, that most vampires live alone. But some do crave the companionship they remember from when they were mortal. These vampires are able to set aside their differences and form what are known as family groups. A vampire family is always led by a vampire lord. This is usually a patriarch vampire, or at least the eldest of the group. Several younger vampires serve the vampire lord, fulfilling wishes, hunting prey, or simply providing regular entertainment by way of conversation, music, and games.

A vampire lord can be male or female.

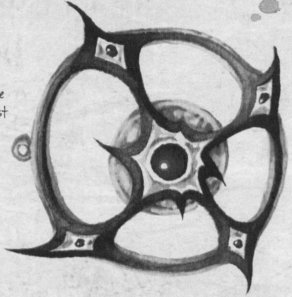

This particular medallion denotes allegiance to the vampire lord known as Culiac. A most terrifying creature, indeed.

Note the blood red gemstones. Legend has it that Culiac was a wizard in life and he forged these stones from the blood of a dragon.

Vampire families are very rarely made up of individuals who were related when they were mortal. More often a vampire lord living in a large, drafty manor, will seek out vampires it finds entertaining or useful in some way and invite them to take up residence with it. In some cases, a diabolically ambitious vampire lord will create a family group solely for the purpose of creating an alliance of like-minded, powerful vampires. These groups are truly formidable and often unbeatable. All but the most seasoned vampire hunters should avoid family groups at all costs!

The family group is only as strong as its leader, however. If the vampire lord is killed, or if it decides to hibernate, the group breaks up and the vampires within the family continue their lives alone or go off and create family groups of their own.

I have encountered only one such instance of a vampire group made up of a mother, father, and one teenage child who all inhabited their ancestral home.

The more powerful the vampire lord, the more powerful the vampires it can create.

Vampire Communication

Although vampires don't generally enjoy the company of others of their kind, they do have occasion to speak among themselves in a language understood only by other vampires. The language is also freely spoken in vampire family groups. The following is a list of basic vampiric phrases. Some vampire hunters learn this language in order to pose as a vampire and gain the trust of their prey. But it must be used with extreme caution and confidence. If a vampire discovers the ruse, its revenge will be great.

Most vampires are also fluent in Common, and any language they spoke as a mortal, e.g. Elvish, Dwarvish etc.

Basic Vampiric Phrases

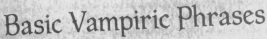

Is it night yet?
E deja noapte?
(Eh DayJAH NOPtay)

I am going to sleep now.
Ma duc la culcare.
(Mah dook lah coolCARray)

I must feed.
Trebuie sa mananc.
(TREbooyah suh mahNUK)

Fetch me my robes.
Adu-mi hainele.
(ADOOM HIneLAY)

Tell me how wonderful I look.
Spune-mi cat de minunat arat.
(SpoonNAYme ket day MEEnoonat ahRET)

Stay away from my coffin.
Nu te apropia de sicriul meu.
(Noo tay ahpropiAH day see creeOOL mayOH)

Whose turn is it to find tonight's meal?
Cine trebuie sa gaseasca mancare in seara asta?
(ChiNAY TREbooyah suh gassessKAH manKARay in sehRAH AStah)

Shut up!
Taci!
(Tahch!)

That's mine!
E a mea!
(Eh ah may!)

Would you like to play a game?
Vrei sa joci ceva?
(Vray suh jeuch cheVAH)

Get out of my room.
Afara din camera mea.
(Ah farah deen CAHmera mayAH)

Stand back or you will be sorry.
Nu te baga sau o sa-ti para rau.
(New tay BAHgah sow oh setzPARah rahow)

Body Language

Like most creatures, vampires sometimes use gestures and expressions to communicate more clearly and honestly than words. Each individual has its own unique body language, so it's best not to make any assumptions when dealing with a vampire. But the following are some commonly used gestures that will serve as a starting point in your understanding of vampire communication.

Vampires rarely laugh!

Raised eyebrow: The vampire is amused.

Smiling (baring teeth): Watch out! This expression does not indicate amusement. The vampire is hungry, and it has locked onto a prospective victim.

Raised index finger (showing long fingernail): A sign that the vampire is preparing to use its legendary charm.

Glowing red eyes: The vampire is angry and growing angrier!

Crossed arms: The vampire feels threatened.

Peeling, extremely pale skin: Indicates a starving vampire. Stay away!

In family groups with especially strong ties, vampires can also communicate telepathically.

Training Games

Although vampires do not enjoy socializing enough to participate in games for pleasure, they do consider games essential for training fledgling vampires. A vampire's first experiences with its supernatural powers can be awkward and sometimes even dangerous, so most elder vampires recommend exercises to help the newly converted gain mastery of its abilities. *They can also help a vampire lord identify strengths and weaknesses within its flock.*

Strahd Says

Fledgling vampires practice their hypnotic powers of persuasion over other creatures when playing this game. A vampire gathers a group of victims. The victims stand in a line facing the vampire from about thirty feet away. The vampire plays the role of Strahd and commands victims to perform some action that moves them closer. (For example, "Take three giant steps toward me!" or "Crawl through that mud puddle.") The victims must obey all commands—the more unpleasant the better. The last person to reach "Strahd" is the winner. The victim is rewarded by being turned into a vampire. And the game begins again!

Either fellow vampires or unsuspecting villagers

Strahd is one of the most formidable and well-known vampires. I will get to him later in this book.

Spider Climb

With this game, fledgling vampires can learn to control their ability to climb up surfaces during battle. Its rules mimic the human game of tag except that players are safe any time they can climb up or on to something (a tree stump, a piece of furniture, and a cliff face).

Vampire in the Village

This game helps fledgling vampires practice their stealth as well as gain insight into the mentality of vampire hunters. The vampire lord selects a place to serve as home base. The players (known as vampire hunters) count to a hundred, while the vampire lord hides. The hunters then search for the lord, calling out, "Vampire in the village!" At some point, the vampire lord will burst out and chase the hunters to home base. If any hunters are caught, they turn to vampires and must hide in the next round of the game. The last hunter wins.

A variation of this game tests the vampire's ability to shape-shift (and to remain changed), whereby the vampires are considered "safe" any time they can successfully transform into a wolf or bat.

This game is also used by vampires to create an instant family group! Vampires will invite an unsuspecting group of humans to play this game and turn them into real vampires.

This vampire lord, whom I knew as Tamurra, loved playing Strahd Says with new family members to help them learn to obey her commands.

Favorite Magic Items

Because vampires have so much natural power, they rarely need to rely on spellcraft to improve their strength or focus in battle. Yet the vampiric race does have a number of well-known weaknesses that even an amateur vampire hunter could exploit, so some vampires rely on magic items to shore up their power both at home and far afield.

These items can be quite expensive, but most vampires have plenty of coin to spare.

Staff of Night

The Staff of Night allows its bearer to magically create a bubble of darkness around itself. It will appear to passersby merely as if a dark storm cloud has passed over the sun. This staff allows some vampires, especially in gloomy climates, to fraternize with humans during the daytime. It can also neutralize light spells, one of the most effective techniques used by vampire hunters with wizardry backgrounds.

Mask of Lies

For those vampires who live among us, human disguises can be most difficult to maintain night after night. The Mask of Lies turns the tedium of daily camouflage into a simple wardrobe change. When a vampire places it over its face, the mask disappears, and the vampire's appearance magically changes to whatever human disguise the vampire imagines.

If you are investigating a suspected vampire, look for this mask in the vampire's chambers. The vampire will not wear it when sleeping.

Impervious Vestment

Vampires are most vulnerable to attack when they sleep, so some vampires have taken to sleeping in this magical robe. Made of lightweight silk embroidered with adamantine thread, the Impervious Vestment comfortably covers the sleeping vampire, while magically protecting its heart as well as its chest. Even better, while wearing the robe, the vampire can summon a ring of whirling blades to frighten away unexpected intruders.

If you ever hear the distinctive ringing sound of these blades when you enter a vampire's lair, run!

Cornucopia of Needful

The Cornucopia of Needful magically provides fruit and other tasty treats on demand. For vampires living in disguise within a human community, an empty pantry can raise suspicions among the townsfolk. So just in case an unexpected visitor stops by, many vampires keep this handy item tucked away in the kitchen cupboard.

Vampires and Human Society

Some vampires choose to gamble their safety by blending into human settlements. They may take up residence in a bustling city or select a small village manor and charm their way into high society.

Why a vampire would take such a risk is a question vampire enthusiasts have pondered for centuries. Even the most carefully designed disguise eventually raises suspicions. A vampire cannot remain masked forever. Our best guess is that these vampires simply cannot help themselves. Some continue to have nostalgia for their past lives as mortal beings and are compelled to recreate it in whatever way they can. Others have more nefarious purposes, feeling that the closeness to human society will allow them to better manipulate unknowing allies to serve their needs.

Can you tell which one is the vampire in disguise?

IN ORDER TO CREATE A FOOLPROOF FAÇADE AMONG HUMANS, VAMPIRES CONSIDER THE FOLLOWING FACTORS:

Skin Color: The pale skin of a vampire is a dead giveaway. Cosmetics or magic are usually used to disguise the skin.

Eye Color: Red eyes can be masked with dark glasses or magical lenses inserted in the eyes.

Skin Temperature: A vampire's cool touch cannot be hidden, so a vampire will usually avoid handshakes, embraces, or any opportunity to touch another human.

Reflection: Vampires will go to great lengths to avoid mirrors.

Supernatural Healing: Vampires will avoid provoking anyone to ensure no fighting (such as duels or hand-to-hand combat) breaks out and reveals their supernatural strength and healing powers. Those with superior acting skills and magical abilities may sometimes fake injuries and illnesses to appear human.

Lack of Aging: As time passes, a disguised vampire will use makeup, graying wigs, or magic to simulate an aging human body. This façade is impossible to maintain however. At some point, the vampire will need to fake its own death and move to a new location.

Food: Some vampires simply shun human social occasions where food is traditionally served. Others will claim allergies to avoid eating what is served or will host their own parties and be too busy "playing host" to enjoy the food. The most successful vampires pretend to eat without any adverse effects. Vomiting and so on.

Holy symbols: Vampires avoid attending any religious ceremonies. They will select tolerant, diverse communities to infiltrate where they can openly claim to be atheists without arousing any suspicion or prejudice.

One particularly bold vampire I once encountered actually faked its death and pretended to be its own grandson arriving to claim the family's ancestral home. The townspeople were suspicious, and the action eventually led to the vampire's downfall.

Vampire Jobs

Besides changes in their physical appearance and behavior, vampires can increase the effectiveness of their human disguises by taking jobs within the city, town, or village they choose to infiltrate. Vampires are drawn to wealth and power, so naturally they seek out jobs that allow them access to both. In order to avoid too much risk of exposure, the craftiest vampires also seek out positions where they can avoid direct contact with too many members of the community.

Typical Vampire Jobs

Business Owner; Real Estate Baron: For vampires who seek wealth above all.

Leader of Criminal Syndicate; Head of Thief Guild: For vampires who cannot tamp down their evil natures. With their extreme intellect and cunning, vampires naturally rise through the ranks and are soon controlling a large-scale crime network.

Artist: For vampires who had artistic talent in a past life or who use their immortality to gain considerable artistic skill. Allows them access to wealthy patrons and to lead a somewhat mysterious, hermitic lifestyle.

Art or Antique Collector: Vampires adore collecting, and this particular profession can be both extremely lucrative and conducted without ever meeting a person face-to-face.

Vampires may also continue practicing any job they held in their mortal state

Vampire Hobbies

Immortality is both a gift and a curse. While knowing you will live forever allows freedom from fear, it also can create extreme boredom. Many vampires stave off this boredom by planning diabolical schemes. But such enterprises, no matter how intricate, cannot fill all the hours of the night, especially for those vampires disguised as humans. Vampires therefore have a tendency to take up certain hobbies. Any enterprising vampire hunter knows that these particular hobbies are an early sign that there may be a vampire in the midst.

COMMON VAMPIRE HOBBIES

Writing epic poems

Crafting multivolume tales

Collecting, especially art, antiques, coins, or anything old

Painting, especially oil painting

Making mosaics

Becoming a musical virtuoso

Playing chess

Illuminating manuscripts

Spinning wolf fur

Note these hobbies all take extreme patience, a long time to master, and they are largely solitary pursuits.

Vampire Banquet

Generally those with a good temperament

Some vampires can maintain a presence in human society without hiding who they really are. These vampires take on the role of protecting the villages or towns in which they live. They keep the villagers safe from most malicious monsters or marauding bands of thieves and animals, and warn the village elders of any impending threat to their homes. In exchange the villagers agree to allow the vampire, who they call their vampire lord, to live among them in peace.

Each year, the villagers pay tribute to their vampire lord by attending a banquet at the vampire's castle, at which the vampire itself is the guest of honor. If you are invited to such a gathering, you must bring some sort of gift, preferably an antique of special significance to your family or a highly valued piece of jewelry. Coin is also accepted, although it is considered a tacky gesture. There is a certain amount of competition as villagers try to present the vampire with the most unique and interesting item. Often the guest with the best gift will receive special treatment from the vampire throughout the year.

The vampire generally employs zombies to act as servants for these gatherings. A gargoyle guards the door to the lair and inspects the guests before they enter. In such a setting, do not under any circumstances bring any vampire protectives. You will not only be refused entrance by the gargoyle, but the vampire may even seek revenge for this slight at a later date.

Menu

First Course
Chilled Blood Red Confit

A tart and sweet tomato soup
served extremely cold.

Second Course
Filet Mignon Strahd

"Selected" by your host, this tender cut
of beef is served lightly braised,
with the juices flowing.

*In other words it's steak
served practically raw!*

Accompaniments
Roasted Beets,
Red Pepper Sauce

Dessert
Bat Bundt Cake

A red velvet cake baked in the shape
of a bat, and slathered with
creamy chocolate frosting.

You Are Commanded to Attend

The Vampire Lord's
Annual Banquet

Tomorrow Evening, Midnight

Castle Dorú

Gifts Required
No Excuses

Travel

Vampires enjoy seeing the world, whether in search of new victims, or attempting to procure a particularly valuable antique to add to their collection. But travel can be rather difficult to arrange. Because most vampires shun sunlight, they must limit their movement to nighttime hours only. Short trips can be undertaken at night, on horseback or in bat or wolf form. Longer trips present several complications.

First, a vampire must make arrangements ahead of time for a daytime sanctuary where it can sleep with the soil of its homeland. A vampire masquerading as a human might enlist the help of servants or animal allies to scout out suitable abandoned homes or caves along the path of its journey. The vampire can then carry the soil in its pack and rest at each stop along the way without much disruption.

Torn from my own sketchbook, this drawing depicts a carriage I once spotted on a recent journey. I have no doubt a vampire traveled inside!

Orb of cold spell
keeps the blood fresh

Blood supply

Soil of homeland

Ship's hold

Some vampires keep things simple by smuggling themselves on board a ship or carriage in the guise of a dead body traveling home for burial. A vampire can easily pretend to be a grieving relative and arrange for the pickup and delivery of its own coffin without arousing any suspicions. With a small cache of blood for nutrition and the soil of its homeland scattered inside the bed of the coffin, the vampire has only to wait and rest until the vessel arrives at its destination. Vampires cannot cross running water on their travels unless they are resting, so this smuggling method is used most frequently any time a vampire must make a long journey via a waterway or overseas.

A vampire on the run from a vampire hunter
may also employ this technique! But a clever
vampire hunter can sneak up on the vampire and
attack it on board the ship

Secret Door

Dart Trap

Fake Rock

Mechanical Trap

Vampire Study

Coffin

Chasm

Treasure Chamber

Art Gallery

Other Vampire Hideaways

When traveling to new lands, or when no crumbling castle or manor is available, a vampire may choose to live in just about any area that contains an underground space where it can easily rest. Caves in forests provide excellent sleeping chambers. Tombs and monasteries in graveyards encourage sleep and comfort. Even the catacombs of large ancient cities can provide a refuge for a wandering vampire.

A vampire hunter may be wary of approaching a vampire in its lair. But you may encounter vampires in other, more neutral locations.

Forests are wonderful places to find vampires. The trees' branches hide the moon and starlight and enable a vampire to hide. You should walk silently—a quiet step is essential for coming upon a vampire unawares.

Cliffs are also a favorite place for vampires. From the top of a cliff, a vampire can view all the land before them. They can speculate which creatures creeping by would make good victims. Vampires also love to lurk at the tops of buildings, because the vantage points are so far above the streets. People of all sorts roam the streets at night, and vampires can easily spot a victim who might perfectly meet their needs.

You do not need to leap across the tops of buildings to spot these unholy creatures. Simply look up. The vampire will remain very still. It will appear as if it is a dragon or a gargoyle, perched atop a tower. The only item that may move on the vampire is its cape, which will billow in the wind.

And with good reason! The easiest place for a vampire to subdue a human is within the vampire's own home.

Ioun stones provide nutrition by magical means.

Vampire Temperament

Vampires often engage in evil enterprises, so many assume they are all evil to their core. But once you spend time studying them, it becomes clear that there is an understandable explanation for what we perceive as their dark nature.

Vampires live a solitary life and rarely encounter any other being who shares their immortal trait. Partly for that reason, vampires care for no one save themselves. They view themselves as superior beings, and with good reason. Their strength and intellect outrank almost any mortal's—or monster's—they might meet. As time is no concern, they make decisions without haste and can spend years, even centuries, calculating their next moves. Vampires who live among humans do not bother to make true friends, for in their view, people don't live long enough to bother.

Though they easily charm anyone into believing they are friends.

Good Vampires

Yes, there are good vampires in this world. What makes vampires resist their evil nature? Any mortal who was naturally good in life and has an extraordinary strength of will can resist evil when they turn into a vampire.

This is my own personal theory, of course.

These vampires may retain sympathy for humans and become "vegetarian" vampires rather than hunt down human victims to satisfy their hunger. Or they may seek out magical implements—such as a Ring of Sustenance or ioun stones—that will magically provide them the nutrition they need without resorting to feeding on human or animal victims.

What Kind of Vampire Would You Be?

1. Your family is out of town, and you have the house all to yourself. Do you:
    a. Invite all your friends over. You don't want to be alone all day.
    b. Curl up with a good book. You love the peace and quiet.

2 You go to a friend's house for dinner, and they serve you a plate of raw steak. Do you:
    a. Gag a little, then ask for a salad instead.
    b. Eat it. You love rare meat the bloodier the better!

3. Your friend gives you a gift, but makes you promise not to open it until the end of the day. Do you:
    a. Really want to look, but overcome the urge with pure willpower.
    b. Peek inside. So what? She'll never know!

4. You're out on an adventure, and your friend forgot to bring rations for the trip. Do you:
    a. Share the food you brought.
    b. Gobble up your own food before your friend can steal it.

5. When thinking about your future, you hope to:
    a. Find a job that's fun and fulfilling. Money doesn't matter!
    b. Become the richest, most powerful person in the world.

If you answered mostly a's: If you were to turn into a vampire, there's a good chance that your strong willpower and selflessness may make it possible for you to remain good-natured.

If you answered mostly b's: You already have the temperament of a typical vampire. If you were to turn into a vampire, you would fit right in.

Vampire Hunting

Vampires inspire much fascination—or much fear—and I will be the first to admit that the impulse to see them for yourself is practically irresistible. Some of you may wish only to observe them and make notes. Others among you may wish to hunt them down and destroy them.

Whatever your reasons for seeking out these undead monsters, please practice the utmost caution in your search. Each vampire employs an array of tricks and unexpected strategies that are as unique as the individual vampire. It will take years of experience in the field for you to be able to react quickly enough to ensure your own survival.

The most dedicated and committed vampire hunters will seek out an apprenticeship with a master vampire hunter before embarking on a quest of their own. Whether you find a proper mentor or set out on your own, be sure to gather the items on the following pages to ensure your protection before you begin any vampire hunting expedition.

Unfortunately, I am no longer available to mentor young vampire hunters myself.

How to Observe a Vampire

1. Keep a low profile. Vampires' senses are much more astute than those of humans. They may discover your presence before you detect theirs.

2. Choose a cloudy night, with some moonlight. A slightly lit night will create some shadows in which you can more easily hide.

3. Wear dark clothing. It will help you blend into the shadows at a distance.

4. Once you have located a vampire, avoid making even the smallest of movements. A vampire will be able to detect the changes in the air around your body.

5. Do not make notes until after you have completed your observations. A vampire will be able to hear your writing instrument scratching at the paper.

6. Never leave home without basic vampire protection.

See the next page!

Basic Vampire Protection

Even with the best precautions, there's a good chance that a casual observer of vampires will end up face-to-face with an angry vampire. That is why you must never leave home without these tools.

These are the most important tools in your vampire arsenal, and luckily they are common, everyday objects that anyone can find. However, I have heard rumors of a new breed of vampires who are no longer vulnerable to garlic. Use caution even when in possession of these tools!

Garlic

Garlic is essential when it comes to getting near a vampire. The strong aroma of garlic is repugnant to this creature of the night. The vampire will not want to be near it. What works best when using garlic is to poke a needle through each clove, and then thread some string or yarn through the holes to create a necklace. Wearing a garlic necklace will help to ward off a close encounter with a vampire. *Or consider mixing up a batch of garlic water.*

A Vampire Protection Kit

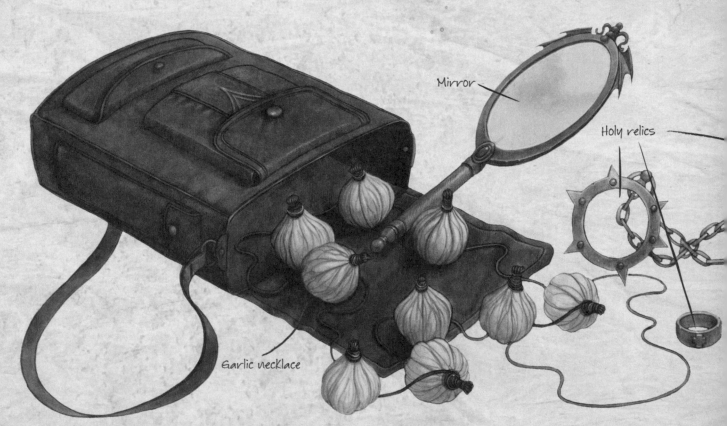

Mirror

Holy relics

Garlic necklace

Mirrors

Vampires hate mirrors. A mirror deprives a vampire from seeing itself. Vampires cannot be reflected in a mirror, and they hate to be reminded of this so they will shy away from any mirror in sight. Thankfully for us, mirrors are usually quite abundant and easy to find. The best area to place a mirror is near doors and windows. In the field, carry a small hand mirror that you can put to use at a moment's notice.

Holy Symbols

Holy symbols can also be used to fend off a vampire. However, there is a catch. It is not enough to simply display the object, whether as jewelry or brandished like a sword. The object must be made holy by a cleric. Other objects that can be blessed include candles and incense. And don't forget holy water! When dashed over a vampire, holy water will leave smoking scratches that will temporarily debilitate the beast.

A stake

Journal with pen for notes

Flint for lighting fires

Magical Protection

These vampire hunting tools may be a bit more difficult to obtain. A wizard knowledgeable in vampire lore could be willing to craft these tools for you, for the right price. Or, you might be able to find them if you visit a magical bazaar and find a stand that carries objects for fighting the undead.

Inquisitor Bracers

These bracers protect your reputation as a vampire hunter by ensuring you cannot hurt innocent townsfolk when you must identify a vampire in a crowd. Put these on any time you are uncertain about the identity of a vampire and suspect that your investigation may end in a fight. While wearing these bracers, your blows will not hurt a normal human. However any undead creature, particularly a vampire, will be hurt even more than normal by your attack. Thus you will instantly be able to confirm whether or not your opponent is in fact a vampire.

Sepulchral Vest

This shirt functions much like armor, protecting you from harm when a vampire or any other kind of undead attacks. Lightweight, and therefore moldable and mendable, it easily slips over whatever clothing you may be wearing. Sometimes called the "gravedigger's shirt," it smells like the earth, and decaying lilies may cling to it.

Avoid wearing this when spying on vampires. They will smell you in an instant!

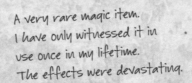

A very rare magic item.
I have only witnessed it in
use once in my lifetime.
The effects were devastating.

Shard of the Sun

Made from beaten gold and inlaid with small diamonds, the Shard of the Sun emits a golden light sure to send any vampire or other undead scrabbling away from it. The Shard of the Sun does have a catch, though. The person who handles the Shard must be of good character and choose to use the Shard only for good. For the right person, the Shard can become even more powerful, allowing its bearer to cast searing light spells that can deal extreme damage to a vampire foe.

LEGEND OF THE SHARD

Legend has it that the Shard of the Sun is so powerful because it is actually made of shards taken from the sun by Pelor. Pelor then molded the shards into the shape of the shieldlike protective, and it is said that over the years, Pelor gave the Shards of the Sun as gifts to his favorites.

The Ultimate Protection

There are many items to assist you in the field, but they are not foolproof. You must also rely heavily on your wits and your instincts in order to make certain that any vampire hunting you undertake is done with safety. If, for some reason, a vampire decides to seek you out, always remember there is one foolproof place where a vampire can never hurt you. It's closer than you might think. It is, in fact, your own home.

Vampires tend to visit places—and victims—that have shown a keen interest in them. If you wish to protect yourself from a vampire foe, leave it wallowing on the front porch. A vampire cannot enter your home without an invitation. Remember, a vampire will use all its wily charms to trick you into allowing it inside. For example, a vampire might claim to be sick or injured or simply in need of a drink of water. Or perhaps it might suggest it was invited to dinner by your parents, your relatives, or one of your friends. Even a cautious reply may count as an invitation. Be very careful! When an invitation has been extended, it often renders all of your vampire protections powerless.

Your best defense is simply to never answer the door to anyone you don't know. That's the only way you can be sure to keep that vampire where it belongs—outside!

Caution: It will probably also drive away your neighbors and keep you awake all night!

PROTECTING YOUR HOME

1. Mix garlic with water and place in a perfume bottle. Spray the garlic water around your home, especially around doors, windows, fireplaces, and other easy access points.

2. Place holly plants around your doors and windows.

3. If you sense that a vampire is near, be sure to have all the lights on in your home. Vampires do not like light!

4. Vampires also do not like the jangling of bells. Set up a doorbell that will ring constantly, especially late at night. The noise will drive a vampire away from your doorstep.

5. Perhaps the best advice for protecting your home is not to invite a vampire into it!

Rumor has it that a new breed of vampire does not need an invitation to enter your home. If true, this could be very dangerous! Yet another reason to find yourself a vampire hunting mentor before you choose to seek out vampires for yourself.

Vampire Clothing

Vampires love luxurious, fine garments. Contrary to popular belief, a vampire does not exclusively clothe itself in black garments and a red satin-lined cape. A vampire's taste in clothing varies widely and is dictated by its individual taste, activities, and profession during its former life as a mortal. You may come across a vampire in a suit of armor or a vampire in wizard's robes. You may meet a vampire in a flowing evening dress or a vampire in casual adventurer's gear.

Many vampires do wear cloaks or capes with high collars or hoods, but often as protection against light or the sun. If vampires find themselves caught outside with the sun rising, they can easily pull up their collar to shield their necks or cover their faces with a hood until they can find a dark shelter to hide within.

A Vampire Disguise

For those hunters who are truly daring, it may be useful to impersonate a vampire in order to infiltrate a particularly powerful vampire family. Unless you possess the capabilities of a master wizard, you will need several magic items, such as the ones on the following page, to help you imitate the special powers of a vampire.

CLOAK OF THE BAT

This non-descript black cloak may not look like much, but it's a must-have for any vampire hunter, if one can afford it. Quite simply, its magic allows the wearer to transform into a bat. But that's not its only amazing effect. Wearing this cloak allows one to slink undetected in shadows or hang upside down from the ceiling—and by gripping the cloak's seams, the wearer can leap off a castle balcony and soar into the night sky.

At a cost of 26,000 gold pieces, this magic comes at a hefty price. It can often only be obtained by the most successful of vampire hunters.

Eyes of Charming: Imitates the hypnotic charm of a vampire through crystal lenses.

Cloak of the Bat: Allows wearer to transform into a bat at will.

Medallion of Thoughts: Allows telepathic communication with vampires.

Ring of Sustenance: Removes the need to eat.

Belt of Giant Strength: Gives superhuman strength.

Slippers of Spider Climbing: Allows climbing of any vertical surface. Even upside down!

Vampires in Combat

ampire hunters are regularly called upon to drive a vampire away from a town or a village. Such a task is difficult enough. A clove of garlic or a holy relic may keep a vampire at bay for a time. But if the vampire's plans are suitably devious, or if the vampire determines it will not allow a mere human to drive it from its lair, the vampire will eventually find a way to return and resume its campaign of horror. Ultimately, then, a vampire hunter must be prepared to fight a vampire.

And they so often are!

Vampires are fierce fighters. Not only do they have the strength, speed, and supernatural abilities to survive almost any mortal attack, their intelligence gives them a huge advantage over any enemy. Only the most cunning of foes can expect to stand a chance against these evil monsters.

As a vampire enthusiast as well as a hunter, I must admit that fighting a vampire is a task I do not excel in or enjoy. I often refuse to take on any job that will result in a vampire's actual destruction.

Vampire Healing

Vampires can be killed. The existence of vampire hunters leaves no doubt as to that. But killing a vampire is not an easy task. Vampire bodies are meant to regenerate. If a vampire has been wounded, it often will disappear from the battlefield to revisit its nightly home and begin its repairs. Shapeshifting into mist also has a healing effect. So bear in mind, even if you think you've struck a killing blow, if the vampire escapes, you can never be sure that they may not return to seek revenge.

Fighting Vampires

Or any other humanoid creature

A fight between a vampire and a human is almost always an unequal match. But there are some techniques you can use if you ever find yourself faced with a vampire determined to engage in a fight.

Remember, none of these methods are absolutely foolproof. My best advice for fighting vampires is to avoid it all together!

Stake

Vampire lore tells us that a stake is the best weapon against a vampire. Drive the stake through the vampire's heart in order to truly debilitate the monster. Some say that wood, particularly ash wood, makes the best stake. But in my experience, vampires are all highly individualized. Learning something about the background of the vampires you are fighting will allow you to select the best weapon to use in their destruction.

When I was a vampire hunter apprentice, my master engaged in a battle with a vampire who had been an eladrin in life. Any vampire created from the faerie race can be killed only with an iron stake, so he used a stake made of iron to battle the monster.

Running Water

Some vampires fear running water. But do not think you can simply trick a vampire into stepping into a stream and then watch it scream. No, the task is much more complicated than that. The vampire must be submerged up to its neck. This form of attack is extremely dangerous. In its fear, a vampire can experience supernatural strength that it will turn on its attacker once it is freed.

Only the most experienced vampire hunters should attempt this trick.

Light

As almost any vampire enthusiast can tell you, vampires abhor light. If you are very cunning, you may be able to trick a vampire to step into a shaft of light. This form of attack is most effective on young vampires. It is also the least dangerous of all attacks. At worst, the vampire will only be burned by the beams. And at best, the light will burn the creature, and in a short time, its body will crumble into dust.

As vampires grow older they become more and more immune to light.

Magic Items in Combat

Any human engaged in direct combat with a vampire will want to consider the following items to make the battle a bit more evenhanded.

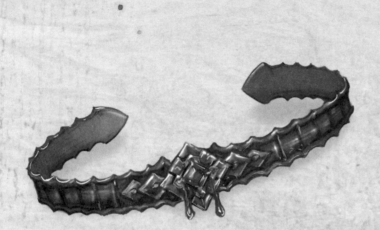

Vampire Torc

The Vampire Torc is worn as a bracelet, and it is used mainly for healing. If you are battling a vampire or one of the undead, a few drops of the ruby's "blood" will bring about the healing process. You may continue to fight while the torc heals you. However, the torc should only be used sparingly for maximum effect.

Talisman of Undead Mastery

The Talisman of Undead Mastery is hard to find, and it is usually available only to those who have proven to be extremely adept at vampire hunting and observation. The Talisman will actually emit powerful spells that can strike down a vampire. Use this wisely! The weapon weakens when used in battle too often. The only way to renew it is to take it off and store it in darkness for a full day before you can use it again.

Magic Rings

There are several types of magic rings that could be useful in combat against a vampire. Probably the most useful of all is the bone ring, especially if a vampire succeeds in knocking you down and attempting to bite your neck. The bone ring does not offer you a means to fight, but rather it protects your body from a vampire's evil energy drain. The bone ring is best obtained through a trained wizard or an experienced vampire hunter.

SPELLS

A vampire hunter with spellcasting powers doesn't have much of an advantage in a fight against a vampire. Vampires are too powerful. The only spells that have much effect are those that defend against the undead. You may also attempt a spell that causes hearing loss when the vampire is in bat form.

When fighting vampires, remember that they have the most strength and power at night. Any attack undertaken at midnight may inflict only minimal damage at best, and at worst annoy and provoke the vampire to an even greater attack.

Vampire Vs. Vampire

Humans aren't the only creatures that vampires are prone to fight. Due to vampires' selfish and territorial natures, it's only a matter of time until a vampire enthusiast or hunter comes to witness a fight between two warring vampires.

Vampires confront each other over territory or food supplies. But more than that, vampires clash simply to show who is the strongest among them. They want to be at the top of the feeding order. They want to be the best at everything. Quite simply, they want to rule the world.

A vampire in battle with another vampire cannot use all of its characteristic powers. For example, it cannot charm or hypnotize another vampire with its gaze. Quite often a battle comes down to hand-to-hand combat, and the strongest or the cleverest wins the fight.

Battle Signs

Here are a few tips that might alert you that a battle of vampires is about to ensue:

- Opposing vampires will circle each other, daring each other to make the first move.

- Opposing vampires will lock arms around each other in an effort to bring each other down.

- Opposing vampires may call up other allies to aid them in the battle.

- Opposing vampires may bring out swords, maces, or other weapons that they might not otherwise need in battle to supplement their strength.

The general rule of thumb when coming across a vampire battle is: RUN!

Since vampires are both supernaturally strong and intelligent, a fight can be a truly spectacular sight. But if you happen to find yourself among a vampire battle, do not stay to watch the combat unfold. You might find the ensuing battle to be glorious at first, a glowing and powerful spectacle. Yet you might also find yourself in the crosshairs, and that is a place you definitely don't want to be.

Vampire Vs. Werewolf

Conventional wisdom suggests that vampires will fight any werewolf on sight (and vice versa). This assertion is simply not true. Vampires and werewolves share much in common, from their ability to shapeshift into wolves to their nighttime hunting habits. For the most part, the two groups can live near each other in relative peace. But at times their interests do conflict, and this is where trouble begins.

This is a particular problem with vegetarian vampires, who like werewolves seek animal blood.

While werewolves and vampires aren't necessarily sworn enemies, there have been individual cases of ambush and attack. One famous case involved a werewolf and a vampire in dispute over a deserted manor that they both wanted to claim for themselves. There have also been some incidents throughout history, wherein a vampire family group and a werewolf tribe begin a feud that lasts for centuries. Often these feuds are sparked by an unresolved territorial dispute and eventually dissolve into all-out war.

Werewolf. [Lycanthrope—Shapeshifter]. Werewolves shapeshift from human form to wolf form at the sight of a full moon. Like the bite of a vampire, the bite of a werewolf transforms a normal human into a shapeshifting monster. Werewolves also share the ability to heal quickly and to avoid aging if they regularly turn into wolves. Werewolves are more social creatures than vampires. They hunt and live in packs called tribes, and have litters of children that look like human babies with fuzz.

For those new to the study of monsters, a quick review of werewolf qualities.

WHO IS THE CHAMPION?

Vampires and werewolves are both formidable fighters. In any battle between them, the outcome depends on how they use their different skills as well as the individual location and circumstances of the battle. Based on the following factors, who do you think overall is the best fighter: the vampire or the werewolf?

SKILLS	COMPARISON	ADVANTAGE
STRENGTH		WEREWOLF
SPEED		VAMPIRE
INTELLIGENCE		TIE

BATTLE LOCATION	COMPARISON	ADVANTAGE
FOREST OR CLIFF	*Werewolves can't climb, but vampires can do so with great ease.*	VAMPIRE
AT FULL MOON		WEREWOLF

Animal Allies

If for some reason a battle is too big for one vampire, the monster has the ability to call upon the assistance of bats and wolves. Vampires are the natural masters of these creatures and communicate easily with them telepathically.

Vampires do not have the ability to receive information from the animals.

Some particularly gifted vampires can also call under their power animals that might inhabit a nearby area. For example, if a vampire lives in a cave, a mountain lion or bear might answer its cry in battle. If a vampire lives in a subterranean city dwelling, it might be able to command a pack of rats. Crows are another animal that will often answer a vampire's call.

Once they arrive, these animals completely succumb to the vampire's wishes, whether it be to ensnare a new victim or to aid in the vampire's defense. They can be swayed to do anything, even fight against extremely powerful monsters or obstacles from which they would normally flee. They will fight to the death on the vampire's command.

Bat

Strength: Flight and night vision
Weakness: Low intelligence
Fights as: Group

A group of bats is called a colony.

Wolf

Strength: Pack surrounds
and destroys enemy
Weakness: Cannot climb
Fights as: Group

Bear

Strength: Extreme force/size
and sharp claws
Weakness: Can be clumsy and
hard to control
Fights as: Individual

Rat

Strength: Bite often carries disease
and disgusts human victims
Weakness: Too small for great effect,
except in large numbers
Fights as: Group

A group of crows is
known as a murder!

Crow

Strength: Intelligent
Weakness: Easily distracted by food
Fights as: Group

Other Allies

Some people consider vampires the rulers of the undead, and for good reason! Vampires exert strong influence over other undead creatures, including zombies, skeletons, ghouls, and wraiths.

When a vampire cannot find an undead creature to serve it, or when it doesn't wish to risk the somewhat unpredictable nature of an undead servant, it will craft its own demons called golems, to do its nasty handiwork. These beings have no other motivations than to obey their master's commands.

Some vampires who masquerade as humans gather zombies to work as servants in their castles or manor homes. The more powerful and more sentient the undead monster, the less likely it is to fall under a vampire's spell.

This is one of many different kinds of wraiths.

Wraith Facts

Maximum Height:	8 feet
Maximum Weight:	Weightless
Society:	Solitary, Pair, or Gang
Attack Methods:	Drains life-force with the touch of its "hand"
Special Skill:	Responds to simple instructions from its vampire master
Habitat:	Wherever it is needed by its vampire master

Wraith

Wraiths are a particular undead favorite of vampires who live near graveyards. Similar to ghosts, but filled with evil, these creatures tend to drift through graveyards hoping to find someone or something to attack. Like vampires, wraiths detest sunlight. The light does not actually hurt them, but they refuse to attack in daylight hours.

Shadesteel Golem

Crafted from dark metal from a plane outside this world and surrounded by shadowy mist, a shadesteel golem is often mistaken for an undead creature. Until it finds a worthy victim, it hovers over the ground. As the servant of a vampire, it will seek out victims for feeding, trap others with the hopes that it will add to the vampire family, or do whatever the vampire commands it to do. With no concern for its own well-being, this monster will fight to the death or until the vampire commands it to stop.

These shadowy automatons seem to suck up the light. A dark shadow may precede them—your only warning that a golem is nearby.

Shadesteel Golem Facts

Maximum Height:	8 feet
Maximum Weight:	600 pounds
Society:	Solitary or Team
Attack Methods:	Can radiate a pulse of energy that drains all life-force nearby
Special Skill:	Responds to simple instructions from its vampire master
Habitat:	Wherever it is needed by its vampire master

Vampiric Kin

Vampires are not the only bloodthirsty monsters that walk our world. Although none of these frightful yet fascinating beasts on the following pages derive directly from vampires, they all share the vampiric lust for blood. A worthy vampire hunter knows the habits and habitats of these monsters backward and forward. You never know when you might be called upon to defend a village against a vampire and find yourself battling one of these creatures instead!

These are just a few of the beasts I've come across in my time as a vampire hunter.

Blood Fiend

Even more vicious and crafty than any commonplace vampire, the blood fiend is quite possibly the most evil monster that I have ever encountered. Its entire being exists to suck the life-force out of mortals, and though it has the capacity for great intelligence, it devotes its entire mind to planning where and when it can next feed. Much like a vampire, this beast has a gaze that can literally paralyze its victims with fear. A blood fiend is such a fearless fighter, it will not run away no matter how overwhelmed it might be.

My advice if you ever come across this creature? Run.

Blood Fiend Facts

Maximum Height:	8 feet
Maximum Weight:	500 pounds
Society:	Solitary
Attack Methods:	Fights opponents with bladelike claws
Special Skill:	Paralyzes victim with its terrifying gaze
Habitat:	Anywhere living prey can be found

Vampire Illithid

The vampire illithid looks more like a squid than a vampire. With no hair, gray skin, and a hunched over stance, the vampire illithid seems ancient and fragile. But do not be deceived. These are some of the most dangerous monsters you may ever meet.

Also called vampire mind flayers, they do not care whom they kill or what they eat. They will fling themselves at anything that looks tasty. And they are always hungry. Their need for brains and blood has no bounds.

A vampire illithid's bite does not create other vampires, so no one knows exactly how vampire illithids reproduce, or how they come into existence. We can only assume they are somehow evolved from illithids, but they lack the evil genius illithids possess. Whatever ritual or curse turns an illithid vampire also seems to destroy the beast's intellect in the process. They do however remain quite cunning, and they will relentlessly and patiently pursue their foes, employing whatever tricks they can to reel them in.

social creatures than vampires. They hunt and live in packs called tribes, and have litters of children that look like human babies with fuzz.

Illithids. [Aberration.] Also known as mind flayers, illithids detest sunlight and therefore make their homes in large underground caverns. Extremely intelligent, they can focus their immense brain power into a psychic burst that will destroy their enemies. They then proceed to consume the brains of their foes. Or, in some cases, they will turn their enemies into slaves. These terrifying monsters do not speak; instead they communicate telepathically. Although they generally live and scheme alone, there do exist some large illithid cities deep underground.

For those of you less well versed in monster lore, here's a bit of information about illithids in non-vampire form.

Vampire Illithid Facts

Maximum Height:	6 feet
Maximum Weight:	350 pounds
Society:	Solitary
Attack Methods:	Attaches tentacle to drain enemy's blood
Special Skill:	Cunning (surprisingly so!), savage at all times
Habitat:	Underground dungeons

Illithids have only three fingers

Stirge

Appearing like a bat-sized mosquito, the stirge does not seem like much threat to a vampire hunter, or any adventurer for that matter. But underestimate these beasts at your own peril! Though one stirge is nothing more than an annoying pest, always remember, when you see one stirge, more are sure to follow. These creatures fly, sleep, and—most importantly—eat in swarms.

Stirges live in huge nests in caves, hollow tree trunks, abandoned graveyards, and ruined buildings. Although they look like oversized insects, they sleep hanging upside down much like bats.

STIRGE FACTS

Maximum Height:	4 feet
Maximum Weight:	60 pounds
Society:	Swarms
Attack Methods:	Attacks in swarms to overwhelm victim
Special Skill:	Can see in the dark
Habitat:	Caves, hollow tree trunks, abandoned graveyards, and lonely ruins

If you come across a sleeping swarm, tread carefully! Stirges are especially vicious when they are roused from sleep.

You also may find a swarm of stirges hanging from a tree near a vampire's lair, hoping to snack on the vampire's leftovers.

Stirges seek warm blood. They can sense the heat of a human even in pitch darkness. When one detects a passing adventurer, it will buzz up close and select a vulnerable spot, usually the side of the neck or the back of the arm.

Grasping tight to its victim's skin with its lobsterlike pincers, the stirge pokes its needlelike nose—called a proboscis—into a vulnerable area, and proceeds to suck the victim's blood. It refuses to let loose unless it is killed, or the victim is completely drained.

A swarm of stirges can lay waste to an entire adventuring party in a matter of minutes, and will chase the group for miles, if necessary.

Some say stirges are most closely related to vampire bats

Vampire Dragon

The vampire dragon is probably most like the vampire than any of the other beasts presented in this book. An undead monster like the vampire, the vampire dragon shares almost all the qualities of a humanoid vampire, from its aversion to sunlight and wooden stakes to its ability to shapechange into a mist form. It cannot cast shadows, and it does not produce a reflection in a mirror.

A vampire dragon is obsessed with its treasure hoard and cannot ever stray far from it. The beast looks almost identical to the form it had in life (including retaining the powers it had as a living dragon), but its fangs and glowing eyes reveal its true nature to any experienced vampire hunter. Like a blood fiend, a vampire dragon possesses a terrifying gaze that will hypnotize any adventurer or monster who attempts to combat it and bring it under its command. A victim with great willpower may be able to resist the vampire dragon's powerful weapon, but most sadly do not have the strength to fight. Once the victim is hypnotized, the dragon pins it down and completely drains its life-force. Or it may keep the victim among its treasures until the next time that it needs to feed.

Some vampire hunters specialize in the pursuit of vampire dragons, mostly because the reward is so great. Anyone who can prevail over a vampire dragon holds all rights to its treasure.

Unlike vampires, vampire dragons cannot be driven away by garlic or mirrors, and immersion in water will not defeat them.

Not only is it practically impossible to best a vampire dragon, but it takes a person who is absolutely consumed by greed to overlook the terrible risks the task presents. It is a direction that I personally feel destructive to both the body as well as the soul.

Vampire Dragon Treasure

As any well-versed adventurer knows, there are ten different types of dragons. Each has its own specific characteristics, including the treasure it tends to hoard. A vampire dragon retains these preferences even after it becomes undead. If you do decide to pursue a vampire dragon, you may wish to study this list.

Type	Treasure
Black	Coins
Blue	Sapphires
Green	Souvenirs of battles
Red	Anything of value
White	Diamonds
Brass	Finely woven garments
Bronze	Pearls and gold
Copper	Precious stones
Gold	Fine art and sculpture
Silver	Jewelry

Vampire Dragon Facts

Maximum Height:	22 feet
Maximum Weight:	1,280,000 pounds
Society:	Solitary
Attack Methods:	Depends on type of dragon
Special Skill:	Dominating gaze (as well as any special skills that it had in life)
Habitat:	Deep inside its lair

See A Practical Guide to Dragons to improve your dragon knowledge.

A Legendary Vampire

Every world has a tale of a notable vampire. You may have heard the tale of Count Dracula. And of course, there are stories of the Vlad the Impaler or the Blood Countess of Bathory. Some might even know of a vampire tale set in the rainy wilderness known as Forks. But no story fascinates me quite as much as the legendary tale of Count Strahd Von Zarovich. Strahd calls himself the "first" vampire, a claim that many tend to doubt. However, there is no doubt that his presence has terrorized the entire kingdom of Barovia, the land he once ruled as a mortal.

Strahd is one of the most powerful vampires in existence. So great is his power, he has even found ways to overcome some of his kind's weaknesses. Around his chest he wears the legendary Dayheart, a blue gemstone medallion that protects against the burning torture of sunlight.

Vampire hunters have yet to find a way to defeat him

In addition to being able to assume the form of a bat, a wolf, or a mist, Strahd can take on the appearance of a dire wolf, a werebat, or a werewolf.

Castle Ravenloft—Strahd's ancestral home

Strahd Facts

Maximum Height:	6 feet
Maximum Weight:	160 pounds
Society:	Solitary
Attack Methods:	Hypnotizes victim with charming gaze
Special Skill:	Can transform into a werebat or werewolf; immune to sunlight
Habitat:	Castle Ravenloft

I am the Ancient, I am the Land. My beginnings are lost in the darkness of the past. All goodness slipped from my life; I found my youth and strength gone, and all I had left was death. I once had a younger brother, Sergei. We lived together with our parents in the castle Ravenloft. Sergei was handsome and youthful. I hated him for both. In the valley below our castle, there lived a rare beauty. Her name was Tatyana, and she visited my family often in those days. From the first day I saw her, I loved her. But before I could make my feelings known, I discovered the awful truth: Sergei had asked for her hand in marriage instead. And so I made a pact with death, a pact of blood. On the day of their wedding, I asked Sergei to meet me in my chambers. The rest of the morning is a blur. All I remember was that when I woke from a dreamlike state, Sergei was gone. I ran for the garden and found Tatyana weeping. She said that I had hurt Sergei, that I had killed him! I could hardly believe my ears. I tried to tell her how I loved her. How now we could be together. But she fled from me. She would not let me explain. I pursued her, but she flung herself from the walls of Ravenloft and disappeared into the mist. No trace of her was ever found. Not even I know her final fate. Arrows from the castle guard pierced my chest, but I did not die. Nor did I live. I became a vampire, forever . . .

In my days as an apprentice to a vampire hunter, I found this page hidden between the covers of a leather-bound tome in my master's study. He claimed it was a page out of Strahd's own youthful journal, a page that revealed Strahd's strange origins. If this page is authentic, and the writer's tale true, it could prove that Strahd was indeed the first vampire after all.

So there you have it—a few tidbits about vampires and other blood-thirsty beasts that might startle and haunt your midnight wanderings.

If you found yourself suddenly sucked into the world of the vampire, would you know what to do? Take the short test below to find out. Write the answers on a clean sheet of paper to begin your own vampire journal.

And with that, I must leave this lair for my own midnight wanderings. Good eve, my fellow vampire enthusiasts, and remember to always keep a watchful eye. You never know when you might find a vampire in your midst.

Treval Vorgard

1. Where might a vampire live?
2. What job might a vampire do?
3. List five signs that a person might really be a vampire.
4. What can you carry to protect yourself from a vampire?
5. If you go to a vampire banquet, what should you bring?
6. Which vampire is the youngest as far as age? The oldest?
7. Name one vampiric relative of a vampire.
8. What other kinds of creatures do vampires call their allies?

Text by
Lisa Trutkoff Trumbauer

Edited by
Nina Hess

Cover art by
Eva Widermann

Interior art by
Dave Allsop, Ed Cox, Wayne England, Emily Fiegenschuh,
Lars Grant-West, Brian Hagan, Peter McKinstry, Jim Nelson,
Shane Nitzsche, William O'Connor, Lucio Parrillo, Steve Prescott,
Anqqa Satriohadii, Ron Spears, Ron Spencer, Anne Stokes,
Beth Trott, UDON, Eva Widermann, Sam Wood, and James Zhang

Art Direction by
Kate Irwin

Graphic Design by
Yasuyo Dunnett

For Lisa, dragon diva and vampire vixen. In this book may you live forever

A Practical Guide to Vampires
©2009 Wizards of the Coast LLC
All characters in this book are fictitious. Any resemblance to actual persons, living or dead, is purely coincidental.

This book is protected under the copyright laws of the United States of America. Any reproduction or unauthorized use of the material or artwork contained herein is prohibited without the express written permission of Wizards of the Coast LLC. The information in this book is based on the lore created for the Dungeons & Dragons® fantasy roleplaying game.

Excerpt from the Diary of Strahd adapted from *Expedition to Castle Ravenloft* by Bruce R. Cordell and James Wyatt © 2006 Wizards of the Coast LLC

Published by Wizards of the Coast LLC. MIRRORSTONE and its respective logo are trademarks of Wizards of the Coast LLC in the U.S.A. and other countries.
Printed in the U.S.A.

First Printing: September 2009

9 8 7 6 5 4 3 2 1

ISBN: 978-0-7869-5243-4
620-2420500-001-EN

Library of Congress Cataloging-in-Publication Data

A practical guide to vampires / compiled by Treval Vorgard.
p. cm.
ISBN 978-0-7869-5243-4
1. Vampires--Juvenile literature. I. Vorgard, Treval.
BF1556.P73 2009
398'.45--dc22
2009016152

U.S., CANADA, ASIA, PACIFIC,
& LATIN AMERICA
Wizards of the Coast LLC
P.O. Box 707
Renton, WA 98057-0707
+1-800-324-6496

EUROPEAN HEADQUARTERS
Hasbro UK Ltd
Caswell Way
Newport, Gwent NP9 0YH
GREAT BRITAIN
Please keep this address for
your records.

GET READY FOR ADVENTURES OF YOUR OWN

A PRACTICAL GUIDE TO **DRAGONS**

A PRACTICAL GUIDE TO **MONSTERS**

A PRACTICAL GUIDE TO **WIZARDRY**

A PRACTICAL GUIDE TO **DRAGON RIDING**

A PRACTICAL GUIDE TO **FAERIES**

A PRACTICAL GUIDE TO **VAMPIRES**

DUNGEONS & DRAGONS
ROLEPLAYING GAME STARTER SET

KEEP READING UP ON MONSTERS, MAGIC, AND MORE.

Every book in the Practical Guide series is filled with exactly the kind of stuff you need to know when you're a hero.

Then grab some friends and go on adventures with the **Dungeons & Dragons®** *Roleplaying Game Starter Set*—it's got everything you need to start your career as a heroic adventurer.

DISCOVER THEM ALL AT YOUR FAVORITE BOOKSTORE.

MIRRORSTONE   **DUNGEONS & DRAGONS**   mirrorstonebooks.com